THIS BOOK BELONGS TO

. . . .

. . . .

I celebrated World Book Day 2022
with this gift from my local bookseller
and Penguin Random House.

It's World Book Day, and the Squirrels are dressed up as characters from their favourite books.
What wonderful costumes, Squirrels.

HEY, DUGGEE! WHO ARE YOU GOING TO DRESS UP AS?

Duggee needs some help deciding.
"We'll help you, Duggee," say the Squirrels.

So, Squirrels, should
Duggee dress up as . . .

a wizard from a *magic* book?

AH-POOF!

NO.

Little Bo-Peep
from a *nursery*
rhyme book?

NO.

Someone who lived in the olden days from a *history* book?

NO.

How about a superhero from a *comic* book?

YESSSSS!

"Ah-woof," says Duggee. That settles it then.

Now it's time to choose a story to read.

Duggee's not sure if there is a book with all of those . . .
"We could make up our *own* story, Duggee?" asks Norrie.
That's a splendid idea! Duggee can help.
He has his **World Book Day Badge!**

AH-WOOF!

"Then, an astronaut came to help," says Betty. "The astronaut told everyone to jump on board her rocket ship. They would go to space to search for water!"

"They didn't find any water,"
says Norrie. "But they *did* find –"

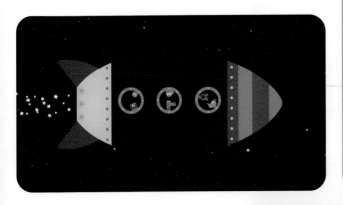

"But a clown grabbed
the potatoes!" adds Tag.
"And he started to juggle."

"When they were ready to fly home, the rocket ship's engine wouldn't start," says Betty.

"Suddenly, they heard footsteps," says Happy.

"SUPER DUGGEE!" shouts Betty.

"Super Duggee used his lightning powers to fix the rocket ship," says Tag. "Then, they blasted back home and landed with a –"

"**SPLASH!**" shouts Happy.
"They found water! Hooray!"
"THE END!" adds Roly.

AH-WOOF!

Haven't the Squirrels done well today, Duggee? They have
definitely earned their **World Book Day Badges**.

Now there's just time for one last thing . . .

"DUGGEE HUG!"

Happy World Book Day, Squirrels!

Happy World Book Day!

As a charity, our mission is to encourage every child and young person to enjoy reading, and to have a book of their own.

Everyone is a reader — that includes you!

Whether you enjoy **comics**, fact books, adventure stories, **recipes** – books are for everyone and every book counts.

On **World Book Day** everyone comes together to have **FUN** reading. Talking about and sharing books with your friends and family makes reading even more memorable and magic.

World Book Day® is a registered charity sponsored by National Book Tokens.

WORLD BOOK DAY®
3 MARCH 2022

Where will your **reading journey** take you next?

1 Take a trip to your local bookshop
Brimming with brilliant books and helpful booksellers to share awesome reading recommendations, bookshops are magical places. You can even enjoy booky events and meet your favourite authors and illustrators!

Find your nearest bookseller at
booksaremybag.com/Home

2 Join your local library
A world awaits you in your local library – that place where all the books you could ever want to read awaits. Even better, you can borrow them for **FREE**! Libraries can offer expert advice on what to read next, as well as free family reading events.

Find your local library at
gov.uk/local-library-services

Scan here to visit our website!

3 Check out the World Book Day website
Looking for reading tips, advice and inspiration? There is so much to discover at worldbookday.com/getreading, packed with book recommendations, fun activities, audiobooks, and videos to enjoy on your own or as a family, as well as competitions and all the latest book news galore.

World Book Day® is a registered charity sponsored by National Book Tokens.

NATIONAL BOOK tokens

Illustration by Allen Fatimaharan © 2021